Lightning Bug Thunder

Lightning Bug Thunder

Story by Katie Burke
Illustrations by Sheila McGraw

FIREFLY BOOKS

A FIREFLY BOOK

Published in Canada in 1998 by
Firefly Books Ltd.
3680 Victoria Park Avenue
Willowdale, Ontario, Canada
M2H 3K1

Published in the United States in 1998 by
Firefly Books (U.S.) Inc.
P.O. Box 1338, Ellicott Station
Buffalo, New York, USA
14205

Cataloguing in Publication Data

Burke, Katie, 1953–
   Lightning bug thunder
ISBN 1-55209-271-2
I. McGraw, Sheila. II. Title.
PS3552.U7185L53 1998   j811'.54   C98-930990-8

Design by Joseph Gisini / Andrew Smith Graphics Inc.
Film work by Rainbow Digicolor Inc., Toronto
Printed and bound in Canada by Friesens, Altona, Manitoba

*The publishers acknowledge the financial support of the Government
of Canada through the Book Publishing Industry Development Program
for our publishing activities.*

First Printing

To Ian Hoyle, who gave us all
much-needed thunder and lightning.
K.B.

To James — a bright new spot
of magic in my life.
S.M.

Not long ago in a small town out West
The rivers ran dry and the clouds were at rest.

It hadn't been raining for one hundred days,
People were sweltering in the sun's rays.
The trees looked so tired; the flowers seemed sad,
They all needed water, and needed it bad.

Molly Elizabeth and Zoey Ray,
(Girls who were best friends in every which way),
Walked into town on a hot afternoon,
Kicking stones, laughing, and whistling a tune.

Kathryn Claire met them at Smith's Corner Drug,
And held up a jar with a striped lightning bug.
(Kathryn was nine and she knew lots of stuff
Like how to make really good marshmallow fluff.)
"This bug doesn't work," she explained, "before dark,
But wait until then, it will show you its spark."

So Molly bought chalk and they all chose to stay
And draw on the sidewalk the rest of the day.

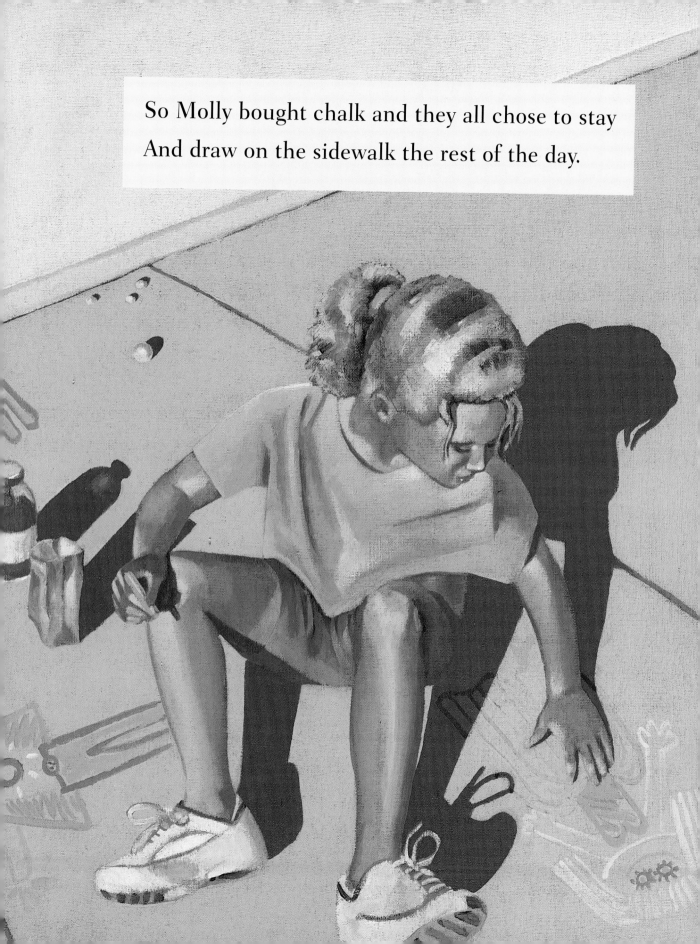

The streetlights came on when the sun was all gone,
And Kathryn Claire's lightning bug turned itself on.
Molly and Kathryn and Zoey all stared
While light from the little bug glistened and flared.
But something was missing; they knew it because
They sensed it, but didn't yet know what it was.

Then Zoey said, "Molly, you see what I see?
That lightning bug there don't know what thunder be!
I think we can teach him so he'll understand
That thunder and lightning should go hand-in-hand."
So Molly Elizabeth, blinking a wink,
Began to jump 'round till her cheeks got all pink.

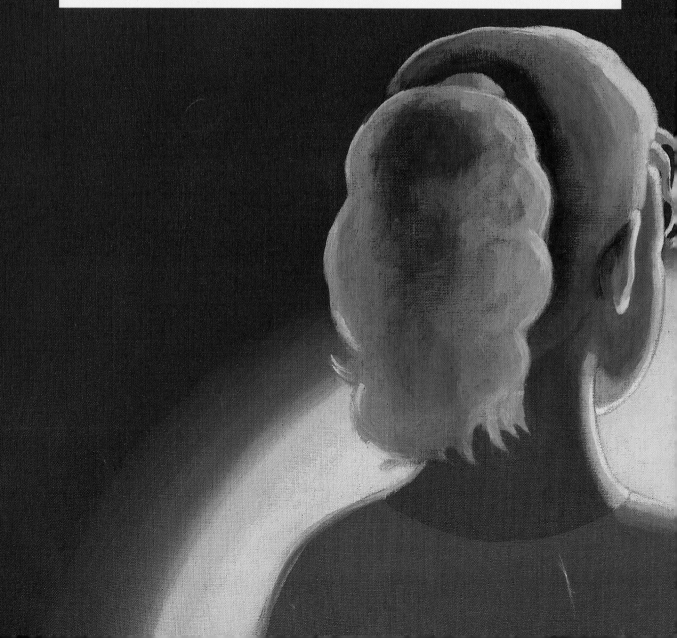

Zoey joined in, with a shout and a whoop,
And Kathryn hip-hopped in a big loop-dee-loop.
What a commotion, right there on the road!
The more the girls thundered, the more the bug glowed.
The shine from the insect was gold and amazing,
Its powerful gleam was completely hair-raising.

They roared and they bellowed as loud as they could,
While Kathryn's bug lit up the whole neighborhood!
It dazzled the girls, this glorious light,
Coming from one bug alone in the night.

Then, all of a sudden, it started to pour –
Buckets and buckets and buckets some more!

"Yikes, creekers and zocks! This rain is too wet!"
Yelled Kathryn and off she ran home with her pet.
The light from the insect grew dimmer and gray
As Kathryn got farther and farther away.
But showers kept falling, with no end in sight;
The hot day turned into a warm rainy night.

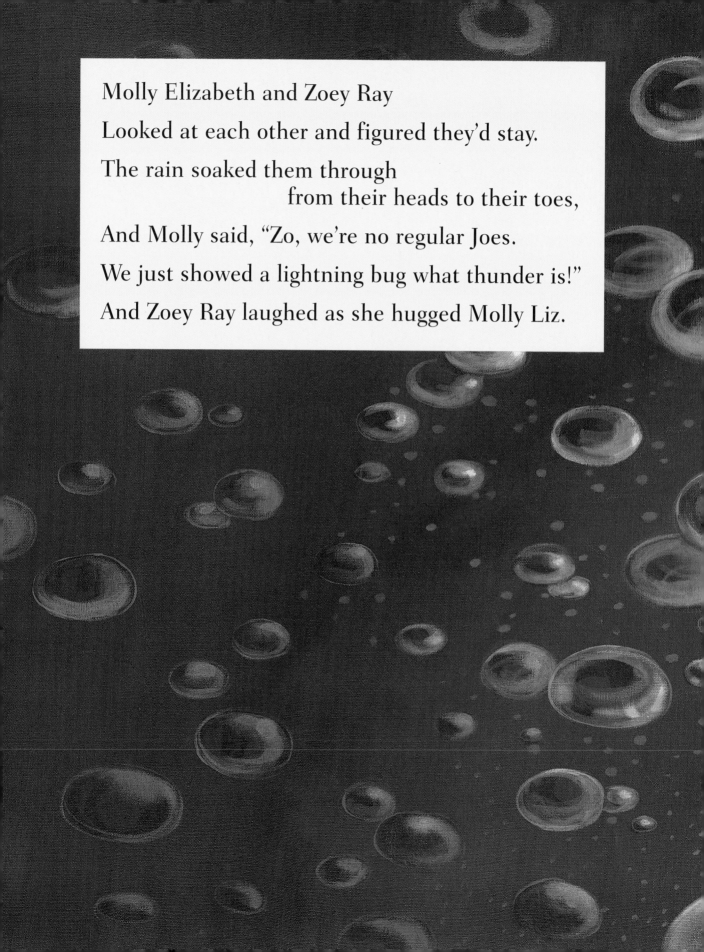

Molly Elizabeth and Zoey Ray

Looked at each other and figured they'd stay.

The rain soaked them through
                  from their heads to their toes,

And Molly said, "Zo, we're no regular Joes.

We just showed a lightning bug what thunder is!"

And Zoey Ray laughed as she hugged Molly Liz.

Today it still happens in that little town,

When rain becomes scarce and the fields are all brown,

That three little girls with a jarred-up bright bug

Make thunder and lightning by Smith's Corner Drug.

And as a result of the noise and the blaze

The heavens let loose and the rain falls for days.